INVISIBLE WE CUT TOO!

PEOPLE *OF* COLOR SHARE THEIR STORIES OF SELF INJURIOUS BEHAVIOR

Deborah Renee Wade

PublishAmerica
Baltimore

First printing

Hardcover 978-1-4560-3883-0
Softcover 978-1-4560-3884-7
PUBLISHED BY PUBLISHAMERICA, LLLP
www.publishamerica.com
Baltimore

Printed in the United States of America

Dedication

This book is dedicated to the ONLY man in my life who had faith in me greater than a mustard seed…BIGDAD, I LOVE YOU and Miss You!!!!!!!!!!!!!

Acknowledgements

I would like to thank my Higher Power for giving me the strength to complete this book. I thank my Mom for giving me life and for always being there for me no matter what, also for praying for me and having faith that her prayers would be answered. I love You Mom! To my partner " RRM" who reminded me that I could "do it" and that I'd better do it!!!!

Introduction

There have been several phenomenal books written about Self Injurious Behavior. The books that I read gave insight into the how's and why's of Self Injury and kept me looking for more information. In my quest to expand my knowledge on the subject I decided to search for material that was ethnic in content. I looked for books that dealt with the African American and Latino adult experience with Self Injurious Behavior.

As an African American female I sought out information and situations that I related to culturally. Self Injury or cutting is a taboo subject in the African American and Latino Community. It is a subject that most of our family members feel is best left in the closet and forgotten. Don't ask, don't tell!.

The stigma that is attached to cutting has affected the African American and Latino families profoundly. The stigma has forced those of us who suffer with self injurious behavior to suffer in silence. Choosing not to deal with the subject has led many of us to drug and alcohol abuse as well as a host of other problems.

While treatment is available, many people in our community who practice self injurious behavior are not aware that help does exist. So, they continue to cut in shame which perpetuates their negative self feelings.

The purpose of this book is to give some insight into self injurious behavior as seen through the eyes of African Americans and Latinos who cut. Many of us started out as child/teen cutters but have since learned to utilize other coping mechanisms as we grew older therefore we no longer practice cutting but use drugs, alcohol, violence, sex, shopping and eating as a form of coping with every day stressors. Some of us continue to cut as adults. Some of us are dead as a result of suicide.

This book is not intended to diagnose or treat self injurious behavior. I am not a therapist, a psychologist or a psychiatrist. I do not hold a doctorate or PhD on the subject. I am merely a survivor of the bloody trenches who now proclaims victory and fights for the right to live without hurting me or anyone else. If you think you have a problem please consult a qualified health professional.

There are many horrific stories of childhood abuse by parents, perpetrators and society. However, pain is not always inflicted by external forces, it can be self inflicted by human emotions. Whether describing gushing blood or anguish, these essays portray the symbols of pain.

To be able to survive and attempt to address the process to heal from such abuses is esteemed. Moreover, to be able to write about it to help self and others is profound. Such is the nature of this book.

There are many stories that go untold, but these brave authors candidly and vividly share their personal stories. Their stories are not easy to read but leave a lasting impression.

Wandra F. Chenault, LCSW

Deb

I don't want to start this book off with a lot of bullshit! I cut because I felt that I had every reason too! I cut because I was damn mad at the shit that had happened to me during my life. Some shit I allowed and was a willing participant in, and other shit I had no control over!

I am the eldest of three children and my mom is my hero. I say that because she was the victim of domestic violence and back then women just dealt with it. I can remember her coming into my bedroom crying with her face swollen. I remember her pushing the dresser in front of the bedroom door to barricade us in from my father. I also remember that when she had had enough she divorced his ass. It took a lot of courage for her to do that because she then became an unemployed single mom with three small children.

Anyway, while they were still married I was sexually molested by my step brother when I was about five or six (my father had children prior to marrying my mother). I told no one! I was afraid too. He said he would tell everyone that it was my entire fault and besides my father would believe him because he was older. So, I dealt with it.

My step brother visited during the summer months just as school was letting out for summer vacation. I remember the first time he arrived I was so happy because he took me to school. My BIG brother who happened to be very cute took me to school and then picked me up at the end of the day. I remember how all of the bigger girls flocked around me because they wanted me to introduce them. I became an overnight celebrity and my brother didn't seem to mind the attention either. I had no idea what was waiting for me when we returned home. The sexual abuse from my step brother went on every time he visited us and I never told a soul. I look back in retrospect and laugh because no one ever suspected a thing. Being the oldest of three comes with a lot of responsibility so when my parents divorced I really had to get my "Big Sister" act in gear.

My mom could depend on me come hell or high water which is something that I still take pride in today, being dependable. She went to work full time and raised three kids on her own until she would eventually go on to meet and then marry her soul mate. My step dad "JAMES H. DAVIS". He is the only FATHER I know. I admired him a great deal because as a child I could not understand why he fell in love with my mom, a woman with three kids. He loved her three kids as if they were his own flesh and blood. I don't think they make men like that today. That is just my opinion so guys don't get bent out of shape.

During that time of my life I had never felt that I was good enough or smart enough or pretty enough. I had always seen myself as being unattractive with big feet and a flat nose. Gee, who would want to be around someone like me? My mom and dad of course told me that I was the prettiest and the smartest. They saw in me what I didn't see and never saw in myself back then. And although my parents gave me positive reinforcement, they also reminded me that beauty was only skin deep and that intelligence went along way.

I learned at a very early age to hide my feelings and conceal my emotions. I learned that children were seen and not heard. I remember feeling like I never really fit in with the other kids, my skin was too light, my hair was too long, I was too square and I had a family that cared about me. You're confused now aren't you? Yes, I had all of the important things, a family with a mom and dad, food to eat, a roof over my head, clothes to wear, medical and dental care when needed, birthday parties, tooth fairies, etc., etc. I had everything I needed; I just didn't have what I wanted ACCEPTANCE.

I always felt like the outcast. Some folks said that I spoke too proper to be a black girl that came from the projects on Pleasant Avenue. I was the girl that most of my friends wanted to be. If only they had known about the dark rage that flowed inside my veins. A rage that was so deadly that it surfaced even when things appeared to be going well for me. I was consumed in exhibiting total perfection. This meant that I was always on my best behavior, I smiled even when I didn't want too, I enunciated every word when speaking and I had excellent table manners. I don't know how the hell I'm not in some mental institution now. Perfection is the mother of all that is twisted, warped and totally insane.

Everyday of my life back then that I can remember, I went to great lengths to be someone whom I was not. Everyday I portrayed this happy go lucky person that had not a care in the world. I was optimistic about the most ridiculous situations and circumstances. I was the one that you saw upon arrival at the reception desk because I knew how to drum up a hearty,

"Good Morning" with the most sincere smile and wished you a "Great Day" as you left.

In recovery I learned the phrase "fake it til you make it". Well, I guess you could say that I had been doing that most of my life. I'm so glad I've stopped faking it. Now I'm making it!!!!

Self injury, cutting was a way to escape from me. You can never know what it felt like to make that first cut! If you are reading this and have been there before then you know. For those that have never experienced a "cutting orgasm", hang on.

Everything was great except for when I got angry. I didn't know why I got angry, I just sometimes did. My parents of course expected nothing but great things from me and when I fell short I would punish myself. I WOULD PUNISH MYSELF… they didn't punish me. My mom and dad gave me encouragement and if I fell short they would always tell me to do better next time. I didn't hear their encouraging words. In my head I heard, "You are a failure and you won't amount to anything". I felt like I was just never good enough, no matter how hard I tried?

I was a pretty good kid never really wanting to upset the status quo. I went to school, came home did homework and did my chores on the weekend. I had friends that I associated with, however, most of the time I felt uncomfortable around them. I was the LIGHT SKIN girl with the long hair and most people only knew me because I was so and so's sister. I oftentimes felt like I had no identity. I felt bland and wanted desperately to blend into society. No one in my family had any idea how unhappy I was about the way I looked. I hated my skin color and I hated having long hair.

As an adolescent I experienced bouts of anger and rage. I dealt with this rage by constantly punching myself in the stomach, legs, head and face. I was careful when beating up my face because I did not want my mom to ask questions about the red marks or bruises.

As a result of being sexually molested by my step brother and sexually assaulted at age 18 in the stairway of the apartment building my family lived in, I would forever feel worthless and dirty. I began to wash my genitals so hard that the area would be raw and red. I wanted to rid myself of the uncomfortable feeling of being violated. The washing became a ritual for me, almost an obsession. As my genital area burned and often times bled, I had a sense of feeling safe like I could carry on with my life and I was clean!

Eventually, I graduated from high school and moved out of my parent's house at age of 19 to their dismay. I wanted to find out who I was and what my purpose in this world was. I had an apartment and worked full time as I had dropped out of college. I met someone whom I thought I loved and we lived together. That's when all the anger started to really show it self. I had had fits of rage while living at home with my parents but I guess because of my moms no nonsense attitude toward suicide and stuff like that, I tried very hard to hide my self destructive behavior there. Now I could act out and get the attention I thought I deserved!

Was I seeking attention, or love, or approval? I had no clue at the time. I got into a heated argument with the person I lived with and I felt like I wanted to hurt her. In fact I wanted to fucking kill her. In the midst of feeling that I realized that if I did hit her I would kill her. So I opted for the next best thing, I turned my attention, rage and anger to a floor length dressing mirror. I took my right fist and punched right through the glass. I can still hear the sound of the glass shattering and see the surprised scared look on her face. "Are you crazy?", "Why did you do that?" She then left the house and left me by myself! I sat there amazed, astonished and in absolute shock! But, I felt great!!! I looked at the damage around me and looked at my hand. I sustained several cuts to my right fist and the blood was running like water, but hold on, the best part is that I had cut the underside of my arm and I could actually see the meat and skin peeping through the sleeve of my sweat shirt. There was blood on the wall and all over the broken glass that lay on the floor. WOW! I had just experienced my first "blood letting". The best was yet to come!

I was taken to the emergency room at a Hospital in Queens, which was directly across the street from where we lived. When they asked what had, happened I told them that I fell on the mirror. I was stitched up and sent home with antibiotics and pain killers. The whole time all this was going on I felt like I was dreaming or having an outer body experience because I was numb. I felt no pain, just relief! I was humming "plop, plop, fizz, fizz oh what a relief it is" all the way home.

I recovered from this incident but soon discovered that any time I felt unsure of myself, worthless, ashamed, degraded, out of control or just stressed out to the point of no return I had the cure. CUT! CUT! CUT! I made a mental note to myself, next time I would experiment with a cutting agent, a razor blade perhaps.

I guess you think that I had to have nerve to cut myself right? It was never a question of nerve. It was all about feeling better, feeling that relief. I equated myself to a bottle of soda. When I was not stressed out and in control the bottle (me) was sitting upright on the table unshaken and calm. When the inadequate feelings arose, the bottle (me) was shaken and the cap was taken off spewing out its effervescence of guts and blood. Ah, what a feeling! It was like winning the lottery only it was 100 percent more exhilarating.

I would take the razor and because I am right handed I chose to begin cutting the left arm. At first the cuts were slight and superficial because I did not want anyone to see them and ask questions. Then before I knew it I graduated to making deeper cuts. It was almost like getting a fix.

The deeper the cut and the more blood I saw confirmed that I had done a good job. I am high and feeling euphoric. CUTTING was like going into a confessional and being cleansed of all sins, slashing my arm until achieving the proverbial orgasm and admiring the blood that ran from each cut as if it were a master piece by Picasso.

As my life took a downward spiral with DRUGS AND DISCO, the urge and desire to inflict pain upon myself became a regular part of my existence. I look back in retrospect and wonder if I was using the coward's way out? Why couldn't I deal with life the way others did. How did I know that the "OTHERS" were not cutting too? I need to let my reading audience know that although my Mom and Dad told me constantly that I could be anything I aspired to be, I never felt that I could. They fully supported anything that I wanted to do. I just never felt within myself that I was worthy of being anything or any body great. I was worthless, useless and looking for a negative place to fit in. A place where my false sense of pride and ego told me I would be a star!

I was still involved in my so called love affair and had developed a strained relationship with my parents. I thought it was the coolest thing when my girlfriend introduced me to people who were using drugs. Heck, this was new for me and I was intrigued by the nonchalant attitude they had when it came to things like occupations, career goals, dreams and aspirations. Hell most of their goals, dreams and aspirations had gone up in smoke! Literally! Free basing was the Prime Minister and they all bowed down.

During this period of my life, I argued a lot in my relationship and felt that my life was going nowhere. My girlfriend and I decided to take a trip to Florida to ease the tension and refocus on us. All the arrangements were made and everything was packed. She disappeared and came home after a two night freebasing binge and tore the plane tickets in half. I actually thought that I was going to lose my mind! My first reaction was to strangle this person. Then I wondered what I had done to precipitate this event. It was my fault. I was not good enough to even go on a trip with. Of course I had a method that would rid me of my inadequate feelings. I went into the bathroom and locked the door. I could hear the front door to the house slam close so I knew I was home alone. I reached into the cabinet under the bathroom sink and pulled out my brand new hunting knife. I looked at it and I remember mumbling and crying about how I was no good and did not deserve to remain on this planet. I could feel my anger rising up with the intensity of an inferno. I pulled up my left sleeve and made a slice on my wrist. I can still remember feeling warm all over. I looked at my wrist and I could see that I had cut through to the tendons. I studied the white looking stuff that was inside as the blood flowed all over the bathroom floor. Again I was totally content and proud of my handy work. I felt relieved. Then I noticed that my wrist was almost severed from my arm. As I drifted into unconsciousness I was no longer out of control.

Thank my HIGHER POWER that my next door neighbor found me in time. She came over to check on me and spotted the blood that had oozed out underneath the bathroom door. She called for help and I was rushed to the hospital. Of course I lied to the triage team after regaining consciousness. I told them and anyone else who asked including my family that I was on the roof trying to install a C.B. radio antenna and I fell. My neighbor was so shaken by the incident that when she was asked what happened she just said she didn't know. I don't recall the amount of stitches I received. I do know that the doctors had to reattach the nerves and tendons. I was told that I would never be able to use my left hand again. Now I had a clumsy cast on my left arm, from my wrist to my elbow. The date was December 31, 1979.

I went home and again was very proud of myself because I had taken control of the inner turmoil and pain. While wearing the cast I still had fits and moments of blind rage. I couldn't really get to my arm like I needed to so I used my neck for target practice. A cut here, a cut there and I was good to go. Since it was winter I wore turtle necks and nobody asked any questions about the marks because they were hidden. At one point I even removed the cast from my arm and considered re-opening my wound. I had intentions of tearing all of the stitches out. I guess it was divine intervention that saved me from that. When I went for physical therapy I was told that a new cast would be put on and that I should leave it alone. My relationship grew old (about time) and I moved on to another one with the same urges and desires to CUT! When my new friend asked about the scars on my arm and body I lied about them. I went in and out of several negative relationships and continued to cut, abuse substances and self destruct. After finding myself one day starring into my bathroom mirror with a razor in hand trying to decide if I should carve an X into my forehead or just cut a big X in my face starting at my eye going across my nose and cheek ending at my chin, I checked myself into a Mental Health Facility. I was tired of this behavior and I wanted help. This was in the early 80's. None of the doctors at the facility seemed to want to address my self mutilating behavior. They detoxed me from drugs; I attended groups and meetings and was the model patient.

NO one wanted to deal with my other issue. While at this facility I asked if I could speak to a female psychiatrist. This doctor helped me to learn to talk about myself which is something that I rarely did. Oh, I could speak on a multitude of topics and subjects. But I could never talk about me! If I were sick and you asked me how I was doing I would perk up and say I was GREAT!! Knowing deep down inside that I felt like shit! I never wanted anyone to know that I was in pain for fear of being categorized as a complainer. In therapy I realized that I had been using people pleasing behavior for most of my life. I started to get scared because the psychiatrist kept asking me about my childhood. "Have you ever been sexually molested?" she asked. "No never!" I replied. "How was it for you growing up?" she asked. "Great!" I replied. "Do you love you parents?" "Of course, what do you think!".

She played this cat and mouse came with me for a couple of sessions, Later I would understand that she was trying to build trust. TRUST was something that I did not do very well. No, I take that back, I trusted but it was always the wrong situations or people. The psychiatrist gave me take home assignments to do. One of the assignments was to keep a journal. She suggested that I write down when I felt the need to hurt myself. I asked her if she were going to ask to read the journal and she said only if I wanted her too.

This was difficult in the beginning because I thought that I didn't have anything to write. So for the next couple of sessions I told her that I was writing but I really wasn't. The psychiatrist was very patient with me and eventually I felt safe and started to talk about some stuff. I wrote so much in the first journal that I needed another one. It felt good to trust someone who was not being judgmental. I still cut when I was feeling out of control but it was different. It was as if a veil had been lifted from my eyes and I could now see the beauty beyond the beast.

She suggested that I attend a self help group with other women that suffered with self injurious behavior. I took her advice. It was a long hard road for me but with the grace of a power greater than myself I completed therapy and am a living witness to how good life is and can be. I survived. I knew I had to do some work if I wanted to get better and I did! I have not cut or self injured ME since the mid 80's.

I continue in the recovery process from cutting and substance abuse. But I NEVER forget where I came from. I have days when I become frustrated and feel inadequate and my mind tells me to pick up a drug or razor to ease my pain. OR just lose control and tear the whole damn apartment up.

Knock everything down and punch out all of the windows. When I am feeling like this now I TALK about it

with my mom, my significant other, my support group or network of friends in recovery. If all else fails I have learned to just sit still and do nothing and PRAY! I was told that when I have these feelings I should remember that THIS TOO SHALL PASS!!!! I know that I am only as sick as my secrets and secrets kill. Today I chose life.

I learned that people will judge me and form opinions of me no matter what and I have come to realize that with some people I am only as good as my last deed and I have to love me and be proud of me. Today I come first!!! During my journey I met some wonderful people who took me under their wing and guided me through my process. Yes, PROCESS, cause that's what it was and what it is! Giving up the negative coping mechanisms was very hard for me. Some days I still want to die to end my suffering. But, JUST FOR TODAY I want to live!!

I thank the individuals who helped me become a better ME! YOU KNOW WHO YOU ARE!

Extra special thanks to the courageous and inspirational women and men who shared their stories with me and only asked that in return I make sure that I continued on my journey to publish this book and become a voice for them. Their names have been changed to protect their identity.

Missy

My name is Melissa, but everybody calls me Missy. I am 41 years old. I grew up in the south Bronx in a family where my parents were both hooked on heroin. My father pimped my moms out when they didn't have money for a fix. I remember him bringing his friends to our house just to shoot up. After they got high they would nod out and my sister and I would sneak out of the house. She was 14 and I was 13. We would go next door to visit el viejo for food since my parents spent all their money on drugs. My sister would feel sleepy. I would doze off while el Viejo felt my sister up. I loved my sister and she protected me. She got pregnant at 15 and moved in with her boyfriend's family. I was left alone to deal with the insanity of heroin addicted parents.

I continued to visit el Viejo and graduated from getting food to getting money. O f course I had to get felt up first, but it was worth it. I would go home and give my parents the money and they would be so happy. They would tell their friends that I saved them today cause I paid for their fix. I soon learned that if I wanted any attention from them I needed to get money, and a lot of it. I didn't go to school because I was ashamed of the way I looked. You know old clothes or hand me downs from the neighbors. And besides I thought I was dumb. I was street smart though. Anything that had to do with beating somebody out of their shit was my game and I was good at it.

I began living with el Viejo at 15 years old. My parents didn't even notice that I was out of the house. I only stopped by my parent's house when I wanted to show them how good I was doing. Really it was all about giving them some money and getting and feeling loved.

One day el Viejo told me that he wanted me to have sex with his friend, another. old man. I was pissed about it but I did it. When it was over I started to feel like shit. Here I am always getting the short end of the stick and being used. I didn't get no money or nothing. When I asked about it el Viejo said well you eat, sleep and live here, who do you think pays for that? I do he said. It's time you start pulling your weight around here or I can get another girl. I felt betrayed by him, I felt like everyone in my life betrayed me, my parent's, my sister, society and now him.

I was bitter and very angry. I didn't want to go back to my parent's house and I didn't want to live on the street. My head was like spinning and I felt like I wanted to faint. I went into the bathroom and looked in the cabinet. I don't know what I was looking for. There were pills for his pressure, aspirin, a shaver with a razor blade in it. I was crying and I felt so much pain in the pit of my stomach like I was losing control. For some reason my eyes locked with the shaver. I took it down and removed the razor blade from it. I sat down on the toilet and looked at the blade for a while as I continued to cry. El

Viejo started knocking on the door and yelling for me to come out. I stood up and looked into the bathroom mirror with the blade in my hand. I thought I looked like una bruha and this scared me. El Viejo kept banging on the door and the noise was driving me crazy. I yelled at him to wait a damn minute that I would be right out. I felt like I was going to explode. I unzipped my dungarees and pulled them down. I pulled down my underwear and began cutting my pubic area. I kept cutting until I felt better. I didn't have a chance to really enjoy the pain. My panties stuck to my skin as the blood dripped and then dried.

I stayed with El Viejo and got pregnant by him at age 16. When he found out I was pregnant he was mad. He threatened to send me to his sister in Puerto Rico. I was terrified. Although my parent's had been born there I was born here and I didn't know anything about Puerto Rico and besides I didn't want to leave my parent's even though I hardly saw them.

I hated being pregnant and I hated the way my body started to change. El Viejo had another young girl move in so he could have sex with her. It was almost like I didn't even exist. I thought that he would get rid of this girl if he knew that I was not pregnant anymore. I didn't have money for an abortion so I thought that I could get rid of this baby myself. I got drunk and went to my room. I had heard that this girl lost her baby by punching herself in the stomach so I tried that. The shit hurt. I was already about two months. I kept punching and punching. Nothing was happening. I went to the kitchen got the big knife and went to the bathroom. I took the knife and rammed it into my stomach, blood was everywhere and then I passed out. When I woke up I was in the hospital. There were police asking me questions about how this happened and who did this? . I gave no answers. I wanted to see El Viejo first. After talking to El Viejo and having him promise to throw out the other girl I told the police that the stabbing had been an accident. I don't know if they believed me and I really didn't care. I lost the baby and thought that my life would get better. The other girl moved out but then El viejo's oldest son came to live with us because his wife had put him out. Again I felt used and betrayed. Why didn't anyone ever love me? My sister had moved to Puerto Rico with her boyfriend and my parent's were still stinking junkies. I was lost

The first week of viejo's son living with us he demanded sex from me. I knew from before that if I didn't do it I might lose my place to live So I had sex with him. What man would ever want me anyway. He called me puta whenever he talked to me. I hated him for that. I hated his father too! I started to cut my vaginal area every time he, his father or his friends had sex with me. Yeah his friends too! It was like I was a piece of meat and everything human about me was lost. I used a razor blade to cut lines on the outside of my vaginal area. Sometimes I would make the cuts so deep that I had to sit in a tub of water to unstick my underwear from my skin because of the dried blood. The cutting seemed to make me feel better like I had something that they didn't, something that they could not rape or take away from me.

As I got older I continued to abuse my body in one form or another trying to escape from the misery and pain I felt daily. There were times when I cut myself so deep that I prayed to bleed to death. My vaginal area looked like a war zone. There were so may cut marks and scars that the hair no longer grew there. Most of the men that I had sex with either didn't notice it, pretended not to notice or just didn't care.

Eventually I met a guy that acted like he cared for me. He introduced me to free basing. If you know the term, off to the races, then you know that's where I was. My boyfriend convinced me to help him set up his drug dealer friend and I did. I would go to his friend's house, get him into bed and have sex with him. My boyfriend would come to the house when he thought we were having sex and bust him. It was all worked out. I had the dude naked and in bed, the door bell rang and he answered it. Oh shit, he said, it's Rob. My boyfriend began banging on the door. Of course the drug dealer didn't want any unnecessary attention at his apartment so he let my boyfriend in. It was all working out. My boyfriend comes into the room, yells what are you doing with my girl in your bed, and then he was supposed to threaten him and ask him for a lot of coke as a token of forgiveness.

The two men started talking in the living room and the next thing I heard was bitch get out. I got dressed and looked at Rob who was now inhaling a large cloud of smoke. The dealer opened the front door and said don't ever come back here. Rob didn't blink an eye. I felt the familiar sting of betrayal again. I was pissed because I wanted to free base too. I had no money so I did what I did best. I sold my ass. I got my cash and bought my shit. After cooking up a rock with ammonia, and mind you I did this all on the roof top of the dealers building, I lit that shit pulled and dreamed of Scotty beaming me up. I heard the bells and I knew that it was time to start, time to start feeling better.

At this point in my life, now 25 years old, I always walked with a razor. I never knew when I might have to cut me or a trick trying to get over. I sat down and leaned against the roof door. I opened my blouse and with my razor carved Rob's full name, Robert into my chest. It felt good and I cursed him as I did it. The carving was sloppy. The blood flowed and made lines as I cut in each letter. I promised myself that I would stay away from Rob. I didn't need him or his bullshit.

I got pregnant at age 30 by a trick and had an abortion. I was still prostituting, smoking coke and yeah dealing with Rob. He never asked me about how his name got on my chest. He was only interested in when I was going out to work and how long it would take for me to make a few bucks. That night I went down to work the Delancey Street area. I got busted and was sent to jail. This was not my first arrest it was probably the 18th time I got popped for prostituting. I was locked up for three years.

While in jail I joined the womens gender group and was told that I could discuss anything that was bothering me. All I talked about was how messed up Rob was and how bad he treated me. An older woman there told me that I should start thinking more about me and why I keep making the same mistakes and choosing the same no good men. I stopped cutting myself while in jail. Maybe I felt safer in there than out in the street. I don't know. I attended 12 step meetings while in jail and promised I would stay away from drugs and Rob who by the way had not even as much as written me while I was locked up.

Two months of being released from jail I heard that Rob had died from AIDS. I was scared shit because I thought I had it too. I was tested and have continued to test negative. I have no real understanding as to why I cut myself because it is something that I don't discuss. When I met my husband and we were intimate he asked me about all the scars and Robert's name. I told him that this was stuff from my past best left there. When I agreed to tell my story for this book, a lot of old stuff came up. I didn't know that cutting or hurting yourself could be just as addicting as using drugs. I did not know that other women did this. My scars are not difficult to hide because they are out of sight. But now I find myself looking at people more closely. I heard of cutting on one of the talk shows. They showed young white girls. I don't fit in that group. Thanks for letting me share.

James

Man life for me was crazy. My mom is Puerto Rican and my pops is Black. He was much older than my mother. I think they had a one night stand, she got pregnant and he stuck around for a while because he nothing better to do. I had a twin brother that died at birth. I look exactly like my dad and that kills my moms. When I was around 2 years old my pops left us and went back down south to live with his wife and kids he had there. I have not seen him since and I ain't looking for the dude either.

Growing up in the projects wasn't that bad. It was the people that my moms surrounded her self with that were bad. She met another man after my pops left and had another child, a boy, my brother. His name is Curtis. Now Curtis seemed to get the best of everything right off the bat. As soon as he came home from the hospital everybody gathered around him and talked about how cute he was. He was brown skin and had curly hair like my moms. I was dark skin and had kinky hair like my pops down south. No one ever thought I was cute and if they did they never said so.

I was 2 years older than my brother Curtis and I was always getting beat for the messes he made. My moms would say that I was supposed to take care of him, her little baby. One day my moms left us in the house while she went to play her numbers. Curtis and I were playing with matches. I lit a match and threw it when it burned the tip of my finger. The match landed on a pile of clothes. I thought everything was okay and went to the room to look out the window. I heard Curtis screaming. I thought he was playing, you know just trying to get my attention as it often did. He kept screaming so I went back to the other room and there he was, on fire. I didn't know what to do but I remembered that on T.V. the fire men put water on fire. I ran to the kitchen and filled a cup with water and ran back and poured it on my little brother. By then my next door neighbor heard the screams and banged on the door for me to open it. I did. She grabbed Curtis and rolled him on the rug. He stopped crying and his hair was smoking. His skin looked like it was melting off his body.

My moms came in yelling at the top of her lungs. What did you do to my baby? What did you do? All I could do was cry. They called an ambulance and Curtis was put in the hospital burn unit. My moms stayed at the hospital for three days with him while I stayed with the neighbor. When she came home that was the beginning of the worst time of my life.

My moms seemed to forget that I existed and when Curtis finally came home I was null and void to her. Curtis needed lots of care when he came home. The Fire burned his rectal area so badly that the doctors had to put a hole in his side so he could move his bowels. My moms cleaned him and made him as comfortable as possible. I tried to help but she just wanted me out of her sight.

One day as I tried to help my moms feed Curtis she looked at me and said, didn't I tell you to stay away from me and get out of my sight? I looked up at her and started to cry. I'll give you something to cry for she said. She grabbed my arm and dragged me to the hall closet. She opened the door pushed me in and locked it. That's where bad boys belong she said. I cried and cried until I fell asleep. I don't know how long I was in the closet. She did this to me a lot.

My moms one day asked me if I knew what had happened to my brother, if I knew how he got burned up? I was scared to answer her because I knew that any answer would be the wrong one. I shrugged my shoulders up and said no. No, what do you mean NO! Well let me remind you. My moms lit her cigarette and took a couple of puffs then she told me to take off my shirt and turn my back to her. I did. The next thing I remember is screaming, ouch that burns, that burns. She said I know it does. I want it to. I don't want you to ever forget the pain you put your brother through.

I didn't understand how it was my fault, what happened to Curtis. My moms made a career out of reminding me. I was older and I should have known better than to play with matches. She would burn me and throw me in the hall closet and lock it whenever I didn't do what she asked in a reasonable amount of time. I tried to wash the dishes as quickly as I could, but it was never quick enough. BURN = CLOSET. I tried to feed Curtis as fast as I could, not fast enough. BURN = CLOSET. I guess you kinda get the picture right? I became good at sleeping in the closet and going without food. I would sometimes hide crackers in the boots in the closet so that I would have something to eat in there. I played silent games with the boots in the closet, being careful not to make any sounds.

I basically grew up thinking that I was a bad boy who needed to be punished. Curtis became too much for my moms to care for and he was sent to the foundling hospital. When he left I cried because I knew I would miss him. My moms started drinking and had a nervous break down. She was sent to a sanitarium. There was no one to take care of me so I was sent to a boy's home.

I learned very fast how to handle myself in there. I became a bully, a tough boy. But I could always hear my moms voice in the back of my head saying, you're a bad boy. I ran away time after time from the homes and at 15 met an older woman who was living alone. She told me I could live with her if I did certain favors for her. It was better than being in a home or on the streets so I did whatever she asked. She asked me to rob this man that she bought to the house. I waited until they were having sex and crawled into the room and grabbed his pants off the chair. The pants fell on the floor and he jumped up from the bed. What the hell you doin? Are tryin to steal from me? Lucy who is this punk? I got up and he began to slap me around. Miss Lucy did not come to my defense she seemed to side with him. He put on his stuff and left. Miss Lucy told me that I couldn't do anything right and that I messed up a good thing for her.

I wanted to hurt her for making me feel so little in front of this man. Again I could hear my moms laughing and saying I was bad. My moms voice haunted me. I took my switch blade from my pocket and started slicing my inner arm. As I sliced my arm I would say over and over, bad boy, bad boy, bad boy.

I did this many times as a teen to resolve some of the anger I felt toward women.I thought that maybe I was funny, you know queer, because as I got older like in I my 20's I started to reject women, especially the ones that I couldn't have. I started hanging out with a group that smoked pot and drank malt liquor. Then I tried heroin at age 24 and got strung out. I remember being dope sick one day and feeling so angry with my self for being hooked that I slit both of my wrists. I went to the dope man bleeding with no money. He gave me a bag just to get rid of me and to keep his business flowing.

I was homeless and lived in an abandoned building on the lower eastside where all the junkies hung out. I was still banging junk and cutting. The day I found out that my brother died I carved my brothers initials into my left shoulder. This made the guilt of burning him up go away a little.

I was arrested for armed robbery and did a bid upstate. This reminded me of the boy's home only the boy's were all grown men now. I was on the small side and the dudes picked on me. They made me their slave, their laundry boy, their errand boy, their sex boy. I felt ashamed because I was of small build and had no muscles. I felt ashamed for allowing these guys to have their way with me. I felt totally useless. It was my fault. That's what my moms always said. You are a bad boy!

I would sit in my cell after being raped and cry. The guards were not going to help me with the pain I was feeling. I had a spoon from the mess hall that I sharpened to a point. I used this to cut into my arms. I would dig deep to see the red blood. It gave me a rush to see the blood dripping down my arm. Sometimes I would heat the spoon with matches and burn my legs or my chest I even took cigarettes and burned my back, arms, chest and stomach. With my clothes off I look like a crazy road map, like I had been in Nam.

When I got out of the joint I wanted to go straight but you know, the streets kept calling me. I got popped again and did another bid at Clinton. I think that I wanted to go back to the joint cause there was nothing on the outside for me. I think I toughened up in the joint this time. I wasn't gonna let nobody do me no more. I cut my arm right in front of my celly. He was like damn man you crazy. From then on my nickname was Crazy or Loco. Again I felt like a bad boy. I could always hear my moms saying it, bad boy, bad boy. So whenever I started feeling like I should punish me for not doing something well, I would burn myself with cigarettes. I was used to that, remember?

I have cut myself up so much that I don't dare have a girlfriend. I don't do to well with the ladies anyway. As for my moms, she still lives in the projects. I stay with her sometimes. She's still drinking. I guess trying to forget the past. She has no idea that what she did to me as a kid has messed up my life for good. When she gets drunk she reminds me of what happened to Curtis and I feel bad so I cut. My last cut was between my thumb and index finger, it bled a lot. I felt better Maybe I can still get help.

To My Moms:

Sometimes I wish That I could fly soar up above and watch you die your smelly breath that reeks of gin what did I do what was my sin your crazy ways i cant forget my brother's screams that just wont let me sleep at nite although I try I hope you go mom I hope you die!

By James (Loco)

Sha Sha

Ya know, this here is real cool cause ain't nobody ever come up and ask me about me…shit.all dey wanna know is do I got the good shit! Yo.check it out.ima give it to ya nice and easy… aiight?? Check it… I grew up near here and my pops was kinda big time round here in the 70's…ya know. he had the baddest hoes and the best blow around…he drove a deuce and a quarter and ya know.he had da gangsta lean and shit.I was a little girl then and me my sisters.i have two. had everything we wanted…we was wearing fred braun shoes and shit while our friends was wearing shoes from simco and shit…(Laughing).its funny cause I remember wanting some playboys and a knit sweater that all da boys was wearin… my moms kept sayin.girls don't wear shit like dat.i was like yeah.one day.watch.anyway…my moms and pops got high on dope and shit…she also kept the other hoes in line.see my moms was the bottom bitch…she took care of all the hoe beat downs and shit…my moms was like the fuckin enforcer ya know…when my pops said kick ass.she did!!! Anyhow.most of our friends was scarred of me and my sisters cause of who my pops was…so we didn't have many friends. One day my moms got busted beatin a bitch down on the stroll and got locked up…since I was the oldest I had to keep shit tight…the bitch my moms beat died in Harlem hospital and my moms went to Bettys House…you know where that is right?? Yep my moms did some time up there…so like I was sayin I was the oldest and had to keep the fam tight.my pops started makin me wear my moms shit and go on the stroll with him to pick up his dough…eventually I dropped outta school.in those days shit teachers didn't care if you came or not…my pops would get fucked up on dope all day and I played mommy dearest and wifey…I made sure my sisters went to school and stuff and kept the house clean.ya know.shit like that…shit was goin bad cause the hoes my pops had chose this other pimp and now we needed dough.my pops brung a friend to the house and told me to fuck him.straight like that! I was like I know he done lost his mind but I could tell he was serious.so I did it… lemme tell ya sis.i hated that shit.pops got dough and I got to be a hoe…it wasn't long fore he had all a us doin it.people was talking bout us and we was fightin people all the time…one day my sistas decided that they wasn't comin straight home from school.dey had dey little boyfriends and shit ya know… so my pops was like look.you gonna hafta take care of my boys comin up here afta we make dis dope deal…I was like damn I aint nuthin but his hoe huh?.i was like yo pops I aint doin it.he grabbed me around my neck and said he would kill me if I aint do what he say.i don't know what came over me.i guess I was mad at my moms for getting locked up and mad at my sistas for leavin me hangin.i went in the bathroom with the scissors and cut my ponytail off.i used to have long hair. when I was cutting my hair I had sliced part of my ear…right here, (points to ear) ya see it…that shit hurt but it kinda felt good too…know what I mean? Anyway when I came out the bathroom my pops was like what the hell you did to ur self… you cut off all that hair and you look like a fuckin boy…shit.

aint no man wanna fuck no boy he said. Yeah good I thought to myself…when his boys got there dey was like.damn what happen to her…wheres the other girls at…dats when it hit me…if I look like a boy (which I really didn't mind) mens wouldn't fuck wid me.my pops was swole and shit…he was cussin me out and tole me to get outta his crib.so I did.i stayed wit Miss Geneva upstairs… G is what dey called her.she was a bull dagger and non a da mens fucked wit her…i wanted to be just like her and shit…so I went to jerrys den and got my ceasar hooked up and it was on…I started sellin drugs for him.i mean her…you know what I mean right?? Anyway.i got popped a couple a times and went to Rikers.when I was locked up I used ta feel like I was the worst thing on earth… one day I was feelin so low dat I took dis BIC pen…(one a da C.O's that liked me lemme keep it) and dug it in my arm til I saw blood.cant tell ya why but it was like, yeah.everythings gonna be aiight now.

I got outta jail and hooked up wit dis chick I had met in da joint. Man I loved her for real…but she was still fuckin wit men and I just couldn't understand why she couldn't just be there for me and just love me…she was livin wit me and sneakin out wit dis dude.she got dressed to go out one night and I told her if she left me I would kill myself…she said go ahead.so I did.i grabbed her up against da wall.pulled out my blade and cut my wrist…blood was all over her and shit.she was mad…we was in walkin distance from Harlem Hospital so she rushed me ova there.we told dem I got robbed and shit…I was feelin real powerful and in control when I had my blade to my arm.when I cut that shit.it was sweet like fuckin honey man…da bitch left me bout a year later for some other bull dyke and I cut the shit out myself.i guess I was blamin myself for her leavin me.seemed like I was always getting left…my pops got locked up and got killed in the pen.my moms died of AIDS, my two sistas is all fucked up with a bunch a kids and dey mens is in jail…so see.im all alone as usual.i guess im gonna die alone somewhere in a SRO or behind a dumpster. im homeless and I aint got shit.

Ya know as da years went on I fucked around wit dat damn crack and started bangin smack…but I was still hittin myself up wit my razor.my razor was like my lover…ya know…or like a lover is supposed to be.always there for you and shit… always calmed my ass down…I just know that what you see. all these scars on my arms was made by me and I was thinking dat I was da only butch doin shit like dat.i seen other butchs wit cuts or razors marks I guess on dey arm but I never thought dey was doin it for why I was…shit im 56 years old and I aint got a clue as to why I did dis shit…see dis right here (shows me a fresh cut on her outer left wrist under her watch) dis is cause I wish I could git off dis damn methadone.its killing me…the counselors at dis program don't give a fuck about ya.its a 9 to 5 for dem.ya know it feels kinda good telling you this shit cause you really listening to me and like I said earlier. aint nobody ever ask me nuthin bout me.dey only wanted to know if I got the good shit…yo peace sis!

Daisy

Daisy is a 47 year old Hispanic female that grew up in El Barrio, that's Spanish Harlem, New York City, USA for those of you who don't know. It wasn't easy growing up back then. My mother and father worked hard to take care of me and my two brothers. My mother worked for a Jewish lady near Central Park and my father worked as a dish washer at one of the hotels down town. I can't remember which one. My abuela lived with us too, but she was sick all the time because she was getting old and she missed my grandfather who died in P.R. Mi abuela talked to herself and she used to forget things. My dad said she was senile. I don't know.

Most of the time my brothers didn't listen to me or to my grandmother and they just ran wild. They used to tell my grandmother bad words and they used to tease her. She didn't understand English very well so I guess it didn't matter what they did.

I remember going to school wearing hand me downs that my mother brought home from the Jewish lady. I hated it and the clothes smelled funny. The kids at school would tease me and tell me that I stink. I ran home almost every day because of that. The kids would circle around me at lunch time in the yard and call me stinky, stinky.

The teasing got bad and I started skipping class by the time I reached 5th grade.

My mother told me that I should be grateful for the clothes and be glad that she had this job, otherwise I wouldn't have shit. I just couldn't get with that so I skipped school and hung out with some older girls. The girls I hung out with were smoking, drinking, having sex and doing marijuana. So, I did it too. When they went to Alexanders on 3rd Avenue in the Bronx to shop lift, I went along and stole what they told me to. When we got back to El Barrio, my friends would talk about how cool I was and that I could steal anything that wasn't nailed down.

My brothers both ended up selling drugs, using drugs, going to J.D., the Tombs and eventually to prison. My parents didn't care. They were happy when my brothers were in jail or somewhere other than in the house with us. My grandmother was losing her mind and would get lost just going to the store. I hated her and wished that she would die. When she finally died, I thought it was my fault for wishing it. I got drunk that night with my friends right after her funeral. I was having a real hard time dealing with this and I told my best friend Maritza.

Maritza was nineteen years old, three years older than me, she told me to meet her on the roof of our building and we would smoke some bud and talk about how I was feeling. When I got up to the roof she was there. We started smoking and drinking Bacardi. I was crying like a crazy person and asking GOD to forgive me for wishing my abuelas death.

Maritza consoled me and told me that everything would be fine. She said that I was her little sister and that she would look out for me from now on. Maritza went in her jacket pocket and pulled out a razor blade. She said that we would confirm our sisterhood by becoming "BLOOD SISTERS".

Maritrza cut the inside of her hand and it started to bleed. She said for me to give her my hand and I did. She cut my hand too and with my blood running she held our hands together. We are now and officially sisters forever. This means that I look out for you and you look out for me, okay? This means that what's mine is yours and what's yours is mine, okay? This means that we never leave each other flat, okay?

Okay, I agreed. My hand was burning and stinging but it felt good. Eventually, my life went back to "normal" I guess. My dad was mad all the time, drinking and hitting my mother blaming her for all my brothers shit and for the death of his mother. My mother just took it and never said a word. I hated when he beat her because I felt so helpless and I didn't know what to do.

One night he was beating up my mother and I couldn't take it so I went to my room pulled out my razor that I carried all the time as suggested by my blood sister and cut my wrist. As it bled I started to feel better. The burning feeling made me feel like I was smoking some bud or something. I was feeling powerful and feel asleep after that and really don't remember anything outside of her getting beat.

The next day my mother was found dead. Instead of going to work she went to the roof and jumped off. The whole neighborhood was shocked because they never thought that my mother would do something like that. They knew that my father beat up my mother, but hell, didn't every father do that? I never could get over that. I saw her laying in the lot behind our building her body all twisted up. My father got money together to bury her back in Puerto Rico. He went there and made the arrangements and had her body shipped there. He never sent for me and he never came back. I was kicked out of our apartment and went to live with Maritza and her family.

They treated me good except for when they were out of drugs and food. I didn't know that Maritza's mother was a junkie and that her brother was selling dope from the house. When her brother Herman got arrested, Maritza's mother told me that I had to leave. Maritza never said a word. And I thought we were supposed to be "BLOOD SISTERS"!!

I became so angry with everyone. I moved into the abandoned building down the block and began burning myself. I used candles to light up the space I carved out for myself in the building. I would lay there, burn the coat hanger in the candle fire and burn my legs. The pain I felt from the burns did not compare to the pain that was in my heart. I lost my grandmother, my brothers, my mother, my father and not to mention my "BLOOD SISTER".

I felt lost and all alone. I can't say why I turned to burning. I'm thinking about it now and I just don't know. I always keep the burn marks covered up. I burned them to look like measles marks…(Laughing) When I met my husband he said how come you don't wear shorts? I told him that I had measles bad when I was young and the scars are bad. He asked me one time if I was physically abused as a child? I figured that if I said yes to that, he would stop asking questions. So, that's what I tell people now.

As for my life now, well I guess that I grew out of it. You know, after I had my two kids and then the grandchildren and now great grands have come along, I guess I don't have no reason to do it anymore.

India

This is not easy to talk about because I feel like this is my private business. I'm only doing this because I feel comfortable right now and my friend over there said that this might help others.I was adopted when I was about seven months old. I was told that my mother got pregnant when she was really young and her family didn't want her to keep me. I had also heard that my mother had gotten pregnant by her father so the family got rid of me to cover it up. Nice huh?I don't even know if the adoption was done legally. You know what, I think that they just gave me away and went on with their lives. I have never met my birth family. I only know the Arroyo's as my family.

I feel messed up not knowing who my real parents are. For all I know you could be my mom. How old are you?? The Arroyo's had one child already a boy 5years old. I think he hated me because I was getting all the attention then. The Arroyo's were light skinned Puerto Ricans and I was very dark. I didn't see this as a problem until I was around six. I heard my adopted mothers sister Tia Milaros say, "donde esta negrita"? My brother heard it to and started laughing and pointing at me. He started singing,"negrita, negrita, negrita". I laughed too.

Julio then said to me, why are you laughing"," you are a blackie"! I ran to my adopted mother and told her that Julio was calling me blackie, negrita. My adopted mother scolded him but that didn't stop him from saying it when she was not around.

My adopted mother got sick and died of cancer, my adopted father was drinking so much and he couldn't care for us so Julio and I went to live with my adoptive mother's sister, Milagros. My aunt Milagros was one of those church going ladieswho was unmarried and had no children. We were always in church. When I was around nine years old, she made me cook, clean, do the laundry and of course go to church. I was sick of church but it seemed to be the only place I got any rest from being her maid.

I wanted to join the children's bible study and Tia Milagros thought this was a great idea because it would keep me out of trouble and away from the boys. Bible study was three nights a week from 5pm to 8pm and the church van picked me up and brought me back home. I got to eat extra treats at church and the Pastor treated me like I was his daughter. I hated when it was time to go home. Julio didn't attend bible study and I was so glad. He would tease me when I came home but I could deal with it.

One night when I was at bible study, the Pastor called me to his office so I went. He told me to sit down and then told me that he was very impressed at how well I was doing at bible class. He said that he wanted to give me a present so I would keep up the good work. I was so happy. Pastor put a small pretty wrapped box on his desk and told me to come over to get it. When I got to his desk he grabbed the box and said he would give it to me only if I sit on his lap and open it. So I did. While I was opening the present he put his hands inside my underwear. I was shocked and tried to pull away. Pastor told me to relax because he wouldn't do anything to hurt me. I believed him and sat there.

Pastor did this to me every time I came to bible study. One night while I was sitting on his lap with his hands in my pants, my aunt opened the door and came in. She told Pastor that she knew what he was doing and that she would tell the congregation if he didn't do what she said. Of course he agreed! My aunt closed the door and left as if nothing happened and Pastor went back to what he was doing to me.

When I got home that night, my aunt went into a terrible rage. She started screaming at me and beating me. She called me the Pastor's whore. She said that God would punish me for my sins. She stripped me of my clothes and began beating me across my back with something that resembled a whip. She beat me until there were opened wounds on my back. She made me kneel down in front of the saints altar that she had in the house and say the, "Our Father" over and over. I was crying hysterically. Julio came out of his room to see what was happening, my aunt yelled at him to go back in so that the "WHORE" would not give him the evil eye.

My knees were turning red and they hurt like hell. My aunt stood behind me whipping at my back and calling me whore, puta. Just when I thought it was over she took the box of salt, poured some in her hands and while making the sign of the cross begin to sprinkle the salt into the open cuts. Man I screamed for my life. She held my mouth shut and kept telling me to be quiet if I wanted her to stop. So I held my screams in and tried to be quiet.

She didn't send me to school the next day. I guess she was scared that they would find out. My back was really, really bad and she had to clean it to prevent infection. Oh God it hurt, but I learned to be QUIET!!! She was nice to me until my back healed up enough for me to go back to school. Then it was back to the usual, me cooking, cleaning, doing the laundry etc. I was even allowed or forced to go back to church, although I didn't want to go anymore. Everything was as usual, Pastor picked up where he left off molesting me only now he gave me an envelope with money in it to give to my aunt.

I began looking at all of the people in my life that were supposed to care about and love me. I was disappointed when I realized that I had no one. Everyone in my life used me in one form or another. Even Julio did stuff to make my Tia angry and then blame it on me.

One night after being beaten I decided that I could no longer deal with this abuse. I decided that I would run away. But where would I go? I remembered that a man at church had given some of the girls a card for his photography shop. He told us that he took pictures of models and could make models out of us. He told me that I would make a great model. I got his card from inside my bible and called him.

Mr. Jose came and picked me up from my aunt's home. My aunt had gone to work already and Julio was either in school or playing hooky. I got into his car. He seemed like such a nice man. I started crying and began telling him what was going on at home. He told me not to worry and that he could help me. He took me to his house and his wife welcomed me. I was finally saved, or so I thought! Dona Maria gave me a big breakfast and afterwards told me to go into the bedroom and rest. I could hear their voices and I could tell that they were talking to someone on the phone. I was afraid because I thought that they were talking to Aunt Milagros. I kept listening and then I realized that they were talking to someone else. I fell asleep.

Dona Maria woke me and said get dressed we're going shopping for newclothes. I did not ask any questions. I just went along with her. She purchased some really nice clothes for me and I remember thinking that I couldn't wait to wear some of those things to school and church. We returned to her house and she fed me a delicious dinner. Dona Maria told me to get some sleep because I would be going on a trip in the morning. I was so excited. In the morning I awoke to people talking. I recognized Mr. Jose and Dona Maria's voice, but there were voices that I didn't know. Dona Maria came in and told me to go bathe and put on the clothing that she laid out for me.

When I came out of the room Dona Maria introduced me to this man and lady and said that I would be going with them to live in a big house. I was confused because I thought that I was going to stay with them. I started to cry and Dona Maria said that I was ungrateful and could now see why my Aunt Milagros beat me. She said that I should quiet down or she would send me back home. I didn't want to go there so again I was quiet and went along with these people, Mr. Tolentino and his wife Altagracia. They are dead now but they lived in

Pennsylvania and I hated living there. I was doing the same thing there that I did at my Aunt's home.

They sent me to a very strict Catholic school and I loved it. It was the only thing in my life then that was constant. I fell in love with the idea of becoming a nun and told the Tolentino's. They were very happy about this and immediately enrolled me in the convents school for girls who were preparing for the nun hood. This meant that I would see them very little and would be at the mercy of the nuns.

My superior mother was Sister Ursula Marie who wore a long flowing black habit and wire framed glasses. She was a no nonsense lady and didn't hesitate to whack you when you stepped out of line. This is where I began to experiment with harmful behavior. I loved the cross and what it stood for. I was lying in bed one night and I remember being very angry at all the foul stuff that had happened to me. After lights were out we could not talk to each other because we practiced silence. I was so angry and I started crying. I was very quiet and I needed to let out what I was feeling. I felt as if I was choking and I was struggling to remain in my bed. I looked up and quietly I said, "God help me". On the wall above my head was a crucifix. I kneeled in my bed and reached up and took the cross off the wall. It had a metal jagged edge. I lay back down and scratched a tiny cross on my inside arm. It was just a scratch. No blood just a raised welt. For reasons that I cannot explain, what I had just done felt good. I felt some level of relief. I fell asleep.

The next morning I awoke and quickly put the crucifix back on the wall above my bed. I had a sense of I don't know, well being I think. I went to my classes that day and felt relieved. Sis. Ursula came to my desk and told me to report to Mother Superiors office. I was told that Mr. Tolentino was very sick and his wife needed me to help her take care of him. Mother Superior told me that I should pack my things because I would be going home. I cried and said that I was not going back there. Mother Superior assured me that I could come back as soon as Mr. Tolentino was out of the "woods". Well he remained sick for years and I stayed there caring for the both of them. I was a very angry person during those days. I began using a steak knife to carve tiny crosses into my skin. When I carved the crosses now the anger was not lifted until I saw the blood. I guess you could say that I had **CROSSED** the line, pardon the pun. I always made tiny crosses because for me they represented the insignificance of my life.

I was enrolled in the local public school and was an honor roll student. I figured that if I were going to get away from the Tolentino's I would have to be the best that I could be. I knew that I had to make something of myself. The other children teased me because my clothes were old and outdated but I didn't let that stop me from learning. I graduated from high school and attend the community college.

During all those years I helped Mrs. Tolentino take care of her husband and I hated every minute of it. I continued to cut crosses into my skin for many years. I cut even after I graduated college, got a job and moved out of the Tolentino's.

I noticed that I started to cut when I was unsure of myself or felt too much pressure or thought about whom my real parents were or thought about my adopted parents or thought about the Pastor or thought about Mr. Jose and Dona Maria or thought about the Tolentino's or thought about my life in general.

I have never married because I am devoted to and in my heart married to God. I had a couple of relationships, but the guys could not understand all of the crosses that I had carved into my skin. I am Gods favorite angel. I now understand that God put me here to show others that God is alive and lives through me. I used to preach on the subway and on street corners to spread Gods word. Now I just preach to some of the patients here on this ward. India is in an outpatient mental health facility and currently uses psychotropic medication to help stabilize her mental health disorders.

Sylvio

I've been doing this for so long that I can't even remember when I first started. I grew up near Pleasant Avenue. I'm Spanish and Italian and I had a tough time growing up during those days. I think my first cut came when I was initiated into a gang. We all carved the initials of the gang in our skin.

Look, my dad's Italian family didn't accept me because my mother was Spanish. They were upset with my dad for naming me after my Uncle Sylvio, who is my dad's brother. So I never really hung out with them for holidays and stuff like that. I stayed with my mother's family.

My mother got hooked on heroin and she was always gone. I had to mind my sister while she was out copping. She brought different men in and out of the house, all of them were junkies. I hated that she would make me and my sister get out of the bed and sleep in the tub when she would bring some cat home to do scag with. I got tired of it and yelled at her one night. The man she was with beat me up and my mother didn't do anything. She told me to mind my business next time and get my sister out the bed and scram.

That still hurts to this day when I think about it. One day when my mother and one of her boyfriends were nodding off, my little sister opened the door and went down the two flights of stairs. She went into the street and was hit by a car and died. My mother didn't even know she was gone. One of the neighbors recognized my sister and told the police where she lived. The police went to my house and found my mother nodded out and there was drugs and stuff on the bed. They arrested my mother and the dude she was with. I was sent to live with my father's mother. I didn't even go to my sister's funeral. I don't even know if she had one.

Living with my father's family was way different. They ate different food and had a whole different language. I grew up fast because my father was involved in some illegal business and I had to help him do some things. If you know what I mean! My father was a good man and I loved him, but he was a violent man. I learned to be violent also to get my father's approval. I never wanted to hurt any one, I just did it to please my father. When my father was arrested and sent to prison his family kicked me out.

I moved around a lot and stayed with all kinds of people. I cut myself because I used have this pain in my chest and it wasn't the kind of pain you have when it's a heart attack, although there were times that it felt 100 times worse than having a heart attack.

I felt guilty that I wasn't there for my little sister and I thought it was my fault that she died. I missed my mother, I missed my father. I had all kinds of shit in my head. I just cut to make myself feel better. Sometimes I cut just so I could feel numb and not have to deal with or feel anything. I never seemed to fit in anywhere, so cutting was a way to forget that I didn't fit it. I got locked up and did some time in prison for drug possession. I cut while I was locked up. Nobody asked about the scars on my arm while I was in prison.

When I got out of jail I got a job and then I got married and had two kids. I met my wife when she came to visit her brother who was locked up with me. We talked on the phone a lot and she brought dope to the prison so I figured that I couldn't go wrong marrying her, Right? And besides she said that she didn't care about the cuts, but that I should stop doing it.

Eventually I lost my job because I was stealing merchandise from the stock room. I sold everything that I stole and had the reputation of being able to get all kinds of stuff. After losing the job my wife and I had serious money problems and could not afford to keep our pad so we moved in with her brother and his wife. My wife's mother took care of the kids so that left us free to do whatever. My brother in law and I robbed different places and wound up going back to jail.

My wife left me for some other guy and the rest is history. I haven't seen her or my kids in over thirty years. That's horrible right? I've been a drifter for many, many years. I learned that as long as I stay by myself I stay out of trouble. I still drink and use drugs. I cut myself sometimes when I think about how I lost all of my family. I cut so I don't remember the pain of losing and being a loser.

Rey

I never really gave it any thought you know, what did you say self mutilation?? Funny that you ask me about that because, well I never talked about it to no one except this shrink I had up in Creedmore. I told him that I got raped by my uncle. Damn, he was my favorite uncle too! Yeah, I got raped. That's something huh? A man getting raped? Man, lets see, I was around 6 years old and my uncle used to play with my thing you know? He used to tell me he was gonna buy me some candy so I let him. What could I do anyway, he was my uncle.

My dad was drunk most of the time and my mother was busy taking care of her father. My mother was the only girl in her family and when her mother died she had to care for her father. My grandfather I think he had cancer, he died though. But my uncle used to take care of me when my mother was out of the house you know like doing her compra and stuff like that. My uncle was this cool dude who used to sing on the corner with his buddies. They used to sing like Frankie Lymon and stuff like that. When he came upstairs he would be high and he smelled like beer and cigarettes but I loved it. He was smoking one day and asked me if I wanted one and I said yeah. He was the one who taught me how to smoke cigarettes. He told me that if my father found out that I was smoking cigarettes that he would be mad at him and he would make him leave the house so I kept that secret.

My uncle kept touching me down there and I hated it! He told me that when I got older I would understand that he was just trying to make me feel good. This fool said that I would thank him. Can you believe that? When I was around 8 or 9 he tried to, you know, stick his thing in my butt. Man I screamed and ran out of the room to my father.

My father was drunk and started yelling at me for making noise and running out of the room with a lit cigarette in his hand, he looked at my father and said, did Rey tell you that he smokes cigarettes now? My father looked at me and before he could say anything my uncle laughed out loud and said I'm just joking, that's why he ran out of the room to you, he hates the smell of smoke.

I never forget, my uncle went downstairs to hang with his buddies. When he came back later that night he was wasted and my father was passed out on the couch. My mother I think was at the hospital with my grandfather. Man my uncle came in the room striped off my under shorts and you know what happened after that, right?

I grew up thinking that there was something wrong with me. I heard the older people talking about this girl in the building who got raped on the roof. When I asked my father about it I remember he said, son that's something that you don't have to worry about because that only happens to girls.

In my mind I was like Oh Shit I'm a girl. But how could that be I got a pee pee?

Anyway, because of drugs my uncle got locked up and I was glad. But you know then I was at the age when my friend's were experimenting with girls you know? I was a fat kid so I couldn't get any. The guy's made me watch their little brothers and sisters while they would make out with girls. I was tired of being left out so one day I just took this kid that I was watching into my room while the other kids slept out on the couch and gave him one of my green army men to let me touch his private. He let me.

The next day I gave him another army man and he let me touch it again. This went on for a while. Then one day we were alone, just me and him, I told him that if he let me put my thing in his mouth I would give him my truck, I was feeling like a big dude when I was doing this to this kid. When I turned twelve and he was about 8 years old his brother who was older than me (15) told me to let his brother stay at my house over night because his mother went to Puerto Rico and he had the whole house to himself.

I didn't mind because I felt like the BIG brother and I could boss him around. We ate dinner and then I took him for a bath. I did it to him in the tub. He was bleeding back there and I got scared.Well to make a long story short, he told his brother. They beat me up and my father found out. In fact the whole neighborhood found out. My father called me maricon and sent me to his sister in Brooklyn.I felt bad about what I did to this kid and I didn't want to do it to anyone else. That's when I started cutting myself if I remember correctly. I cut myself because I was mad that my uncle had damaged me like that. I couldn't stop thinking about what he did to me. The feeling that he left me with was with me everyday. I tried to fight off the urge to mess with boys but some how I couldn't.

In the beginning I used to cut myself before I molested anyone hopping that it would help me stop and relieve all that pent up anger. Then I just starting molesting kids and cutting myself after. I know it sounds crazy but... I started using drugs and drinking. I molested little boys. I hate myself! Right now I'm in a program and I'm a registered sex offender.

Sandra

Just look at my arms! They look messed up, right?! I used to cut up my arms because I was mad at my brother for having sex with me. I was only six and he just did whatever he wanted. My father left us when I was a baby and my mother was bed ridden and she suffered with mental illness. My brother Keith was basically my primary care taker. He was the man of the house and he never let me forget it.

I got pregnant from him when I was 13 years old and had a miscarriage. I was glad that I lost the baby because I was not ready to be a mother. I think my brother was upset that he had to take care of me and my mother. He took all of his frustrations out on me. I was pregnant again at 15 and this time I had the baby. I cut my arms up a lot when I was pregnant. When I was at the hospital in labor the nurse took my blood pressure and asked me what happened to my arm? I just told her that I was in a lot of fights. She shook her head and said, you young girls!!

My son was born with downs syndrome and I hated how ugly he looked. My brother said that I must have been messing around with somebody else because he couldn't have produced such a monster. My son was eventually taken away from me because I ran away from home and left him there with my mother who was mental and couldn't even take care of herself let alone take care of a baby.

The people next door called BCW (Bureau of Child Welfare) and tell you the truth, I was glad that they took him.

I kept slicing myself during my relationship with my husband because he used to beat the hell out of me. I was mad and I felt helpless. I turned to drugs to also help me numb my feelings. It seemed like men just dogged me out.

I 'm a 55 year old woman and I feel like I have found peace within myself. I attend a group for incest survivors and I don't cut anymore. I take medication for depression and lets see I had a hysterectomy when I turned 30 because I had cancer. That's my life in sixty seconds!

Freda

I've been a tom boy all my life. I walk like a boy, I talk like a boy and I dress like a boy. My family said it's because my dad always wanted a boy that he could chill out with. I have four sisters and I am the youngest. My father is the one who taught me how to protect myself against the boy's and the teasing that I got at school. Most of the girls were afraid of me and really didn't say too much to me. It was the boy's. I think they were afraid of me because I could throw a football better than most of them. I even tried out for the team but I was told that girls couldn't play on the boy's team.

I didn't fit in with the boys and I sure didn't fit in with the girls, I was a misfit I guess you could say. When I started to develop breasts and stuff, I was scared because I was starting to look more like a girl you know. I hated that! I hated what I was becoming! My dad was cool with me looking like a boy but not my mom and my sister's. The other kids used to tease my sister's because of me.

One day while I was changing into my gym clothes the other girls started laughing at me. I was used to this so I didn't pay any attention to them. But they kept laughing and pointing. Finally one of them said, "See she's got her period, I told you she was a girl".

When I looked down there was a stream of blood running down the inside of my thigh and when I went to the bathroom I saw that my underwear were all messed up.

I was so humiliated that I wanted to die right there on the spot. I went home and told my mom and she said, "Well Freda, you're a woman now". Oh my god, a woman? I didn't even like being a girl, now I'm a woman? I learned how to deal with this once a month monster and got good at hiding my pads in my hand when I needed to go to the bathroom to change them while in school.

In my senior year in high school my mom pressured me to go to the prom with the Pastors son. I did, although I would rather have been escorting Tina Brown. The night went pretty much as I had expected. Troy picked up from home and dropped me off at the prom. I didn't see him again until it was time to go home. On the way home he decided to take the long way and suggested that we stop at lover's lane to talk. I didn't see any harm in it so I said okay.

He pulled out a bottle of wine from under his car seat and started swigging then passed it to me. I took a couple of swigs too. He went in his wallet and took out a joint and we both smoked. This was my first time smoking reefer but I didn't want him to know. We were both kind of giddy. Troy looked at me and said, "Do you really like girls'? I said, "yeah"! He looked at me and said that I would go to hell because I was a sinner. He said that women who like other women will be damned for life.

I got mad and said, “Fuck you Troy”. What happened next is a blur. I remember fighting to get him off me and hearing the sound of my clothes rip. Next thing I know, this boy is on top of me. I fought as hard as I could. He told me if I stop fighting him he would be finished in a minute.

When he got off of me he apologized to me and pleaded with me not to tell anyone. I told him that I wouldn’t. When I got home I ran to the bathroom before my mom could see my torn clothing. She knocked on the door and asked if I had a good time. I lied and said yes. She went back to bed.

I got into the tub and wondered what I had done to make Troy act like that? I was confused! I was ashamed! I was scared! I wanted to disappear, I wanted to die!! I don’t know what made me think about the small mirror that I had inside my little prom bag. I picked the bag up from the floor, reached in and took the mirror out and opened it. When I looked in I saw the face of disgrace staring back at me. I dropped the mirror and it broke into little pieces.

I picked up one of the shards of glass and cut my wrist with it. The water in the tub began to swirl with blood. I began to feel like I was hypnotized or something. I kept starring at it. I was feeling the pain of being raped and the cut seemed to make it okay. I never told anyone about that night with Troy and I never ever forgot it either!

I noticed that after the rape I started to act out. I wasn't going to college and my mom said that I needed to get a job. I decided to ask old man Phil if I could work at his candy store. He said yes and I jumped for joy because I had a job where I could dress the way I liked, and besides everyone there on the block knew me.

I was very happy to have a job but somehow I felt haunted by being raped. I felt like I was nothing. When I thought about being raped I wanted to tell my dad but I was scared because I knew that he would hurt Troy. So, I kept quiet and held it inside. I kept telling myself that I would get over it. I never did!

When my dad died I took it hard. I cried my heart out. I couldn't believe that he left me. He was the only person that understood me. My mom never did and she never tried either. My mother and I were the only two left living in our house. All of my sister's were married or living on their own. The day of my dad's funeral I carved my dads initials into my arm. I let the blood flow and I watched it. I felt some kind of peace flow through me.

After that I began to cut on a regular basis. It was almost as if I were addicted to the whole thing. When I cut myself I felt like I was high or something. It was like smoking a joint only I didn't get the munchies afterwards.

I met a woman and fell in love with her. She said that she loved me too! But she had two kids and an ex-husband. Our relationship was good at first. She told me that her kids were with her ex-husband for summer vacation. We did a lot of things together that summer. When school started in September she started to spend less time with me. I never met her kids and she never invited me back to her house. I felt like shit, like I was being used. I called her and she told me not to call her anymore because she was only experimenting over the summer and she and I were through. I was like how dare she! How dare she do that to me. I felt raped all over again.

I went home and cried until my eyes were bloodshot. I went to my metal box, took out my cutter of choice and proceeded to cut my arms. I wanted to get rid of the pain she caused me. I wanted to go to her house and fuck her up but I thought about her kids. I cried and cut myself to sleep that night.

The next morning my mother woke me up. She told me that old man Phil's candy store burned down. Shit.I lost my girl and now my job! I was feeling out of control. Why were all these things happening to me? I decided that I would leave Jersey and move to NYC with the money I saved from working.

I got hooked up with the wrong crowd and got heavily into drugs. I started out selling drugs then in the end selling my body to get drugs. My arms have track marks and scars from my cutting binges. I cut a lot when I got high. It was almost as if they went hand and hand. I'm 43 now and I still cut.

Romero/Ronnie

When I was born I had two sexes. My parents didn't know if I was to be a boy or a girl. The doctors told them to choose a gender and raise me like that. They didn't have the money or resources to investigate this so they raised me as a male. My parents were afraid to have any other children because of what had happened to me. My parents eventually divorced because they were always arguing over which one of them gave me the cursed gene.

After they separated I didn't see my father again until I was 32 years old. He was dying from cancer and I visited him at the hospital. I was confused as a child because I couldn't figure out why God had played such a cruel trick on me? I was small and kind of feminine and all the kids at school teased me. When I was in the eighth grade my worst nightmare came true. I had to go to the bathroom really bad. I tried to hold it but I couldn't so I went. A bunch of boys were in there and at first they were paying me no attention. Then all of a sudden one of them said, "Look Romero pisses like a girl"!

It was true, I did. My penis was so small that it was better for me to sit down and go. As I stood to pull up my pants they pushed me against the bathroom wall. All of them looked down there. They pointed and laughed. They told the whole school about what they had seen. I went home crying and never returned. I felt like a freak and I wanted to hide away some where. But where could I go I was only 11.

My mother tried home schooling me but that was impossible because she never finished the 7th grade. I was so alone. So I spent a lot of my time watching television and dressing up in my mother's clothes. Tell you the truth, I was kind of glad that my father was gone. He used to hit me across my face when he would catch me dressed in my mothers stuff.

My mother had to work and I began to hate her for what I had become. I looked in the mirror at my genitals one day and decided that my penis had to go. I liked the way I looked when I tucked my penis in my ass because I felt free and my dungarees fit better you know. No bulge! I went to the kitchen and took the big knife from the drawer. I stretched my penis out and tried to cut it off but that shit hurt. So I looked around the apartment to find something else to use. I kept looking. As I searched I realized that my pinky finger was burning. I thought that I had cut it. When I examined it I saw that I had a rubber band around the pinky finger and it was numb and starting to turn blue. Aha, I thought, I'll use a rubber band, and I did.

I took a big rubber band and rapped it around my penis. After a while it started to throb and hurt. It started to turn blue. I can't explain it but, I started to feel light headed like I was flying. As I examined it I felt good from the pain I was feeling. I was now in control of me. I would say when enough was enough! I fell asleep with it on and when my mother came home she said that I looked like I was unconscious so she called an ambulance. When they got me to the hospital and took my clothes off they found the rubber band on my penis. I was embarrassed, not for me but for my mother. The rubber band was wound so tightly and my penis was so swollen and damaged that the doctors removed it. They said that my penis had gangrene so I had a "penectomy".

The doctors made an opening at the stump of my penis so that I could pee. I stayed in the hospital for some time after the corrective surgery. Whatever they did didn't help because urine still leaks from the stump I have. The one good thing that came out of this was I finally had a name for my condition. I was a hermaphrodite. A hermaphrodite!

The doctor explained the condition to me. He said that it was a rare genetic disorder. He said that I was born with internal organs of a man AND a woman! And that I had a combination of male and female parts on the outside. In other words, the bastards told me that I was half man and half woman. I laughed because I remember thinking shit I could fuck myself! But this was serious you know? It explained why I felt so girly.

My mother tried to make believe that I was normal when I knew that I wasn't. I remember that I used to rub my skin with an eraser until the skin was hot and raw. This seemed to ease my uncomfortable feelings. Then I started using lye that my mother kept under the sink. I let the lye drip onto my legs where the urine stains had already caused some ugly nastiness. It burned me to the bone sometimes. I was always showing up at the E.R with infected third degree burns.

My mother took me to church hoping that that would help me. It did. It gave me a new way to control my miserable existence. I heard the Pastor say something about if thy eye offends you then pluck it out. I never forgot that and one day when I was feeling way out of sorts I took a hanger and tried to dig out my eye. Hell, my penis offended me so I tried to get rid of it. Now it was my eyes turn. Well, as you can see I am blind in that eye. The doctors said that I damaged the cornea. Oh well! So as you can see I have lived a horrible life. I am constantly thinking of new ways to end my suffering. I don't want to die, but I want to die.

I have no children, my parents are now dead and I have no family. I am an alcoholic and a heroin addict. I have no true friends. I am alone in this fucked up world. I used to have a lover but he died from the virus in 1988. I miss him. He was the only person that understood me. He was the only person I could confide in. I tested positive for the virus too! I don't know what God is waiting for? He took Gill, why don't he just hurry up and take me too! Today I burned my arm with cigarettes. I was thinking about how messed up my life has been and I needed something to take away the pain so I burned myself a couple of times, see? The pain helps keep me sane. I stopped taking my HIV medication and I have been in and out of the hospital. I had pneumonia two months ago. Nobody cares about you these days. They were in a hurry to discharge me even though I have no place to live. I have been homeless for a while now. I live on the streets. Its too dangerous to live in the men's shelter, you know. I go to the Mission for food and clothing. When I had a couple of dollars I would rent a room at the "Sunshine Hotel" in the bowery. It was a mess down there too, but at least I'm in out of the cold. The manager Nate was really very nice to me. I think he passed away a couple of years ago.

Anyway, here I am a lost soul. I don't know why I never went to the shrink to have my head examined for hurting myself? I've been doing it so long it just seems like the most normal thing to do.

After the interview the author gave Ronnie the number to the Gay Men's Health Crisis, which is located in the Tisch Building at 119 West 24th Street in New York City. I hope he uses the information!

In my experience as a recovering self injurer, I can remember that I never really thought about what might happen as a result of cutting myself. I seemed to act almost on sheer impulse. I usually went from zero to ten in a matter of seconds and without thinking I would end up with razor in hand and the cutting would begin. Once I saw the blood I became mesmerized and time stood still. I would admire and examine the streams as they ran down my arm. The sting of the cuts had a healing, soothing and comforting effect. It was an effect that I welcomed and an effect that I was very familiar with.

As a recovering addict I have come to understand that my character defects led to my path of self destruction. When I stopped cutting myself in the 80's, it didn't mean that I was cured and did not want to cut. I still wanted to cut but I had found something else to numb the pain, DRUGS!

In my estimation, I had become addicted to my self injuring cycle. My cycle consisted of feeling feelings of insecurity, low self esteem, no self worth, no conscious contact with the world as a whole, having very little or no spiritual motivation, feelings of doom and despair, a lack of control over my emotions and over others, just plain feeling like a total failure.

I do not have a degree in the field of self injurious behavior, however, I am a survivor and this is where my knowledge and experience come from. I am a "carrier". A carrier of scars and lost dreams in a world that says you have to be perfect. A world that frowns on your imperfections and scorns you, forcing you to hide from society. I hid for a long time!

I think back to my days of loneliness and despair with
an attitude of sullen indifference. Somehow I seem
to have turned my back on most of the tragic events
erasing all that was soiled, dirty and unclean.
Within my eyes, the windows to my dreams of promises
yet to be fulfilled still lives the frightened little girl.
Deb

You held me up to the light as if I
would shine forever. My connections to space
disappeared as my memory burned from
the after glow of consciousness. When did I lose
my aura, my halo of self proclaimed exactness
that mirrored the images of life?
Deb

Shall I dance to music that only I can hear? Whirling and
twirling
as the dull pain infects muscles that are atrophied and scream
silently
for a chance to drink from the fountain of forgiveness. Is this
to
be my reward for remaining quiet and keeping secrets
that were far beyond my years of comprehension? Will I be
saved in the
nick of time or will I run into the forest lost and bewildered
with out stretched
hands trying to fend of the darkness??
Deb

INVISIBLE, WE CUT TOO!

While I continue to save spaces for the entity
that comes in the night like a wrecking ball with the force of
a million demolition workers, who is going to answer for the
injustice that my
heart feels? Is there a being who will claim my emotional
and tedious heart
and soothe the inconsolable flat lining that I have come to
expect hour upon hour
while I listen to the howling of a cat.....ME.... who looks for
milk and nurturing.
There must be a happy ending to all of this because I've seen
evidence of things to come on the big screen where creation
meets
and interacts with the cranial effects I have stored away for
future reference.
I misuse my power though through subliminal and subtle
hints that
haunt and confuse my mental activity. I am unable to defuse
my brain which
is always computing and totaling statistics, comparing and
relating to relativity,
adding and subtracting, multiplying and dividing until there
is nothing
left and I am all gone. Ashes to ashes, dust to dust.

Deb

It is time for midnight when all of the goblins come out to
play and haunt me, making me remember things from
yesteryear that swirl around in my head as if I am on a
bad trip trying to fly high as the moon.
I want to keep calm, cool and collective as suggested
in my favorite t.v. commercial but I cannot for the
atmosphere is not conducive to this marketing tool
and I eventually let them see me sweat.
Reaching for a symbol of hope I grasp the only pin
left standing that has somehow evaded the bowl
of the ball and I hold on for life as I know what will
come next. The knowledge of the alley and how it works
with
its automated systems in place ready to snatch me
up as I was left standing in the strike zone alone again.
There is no winner in this game, this experience thrust upon
me
as if I deserved it for outstanding citizen of the year, it's just
me
as I stand ashamed as a loser in the Olympics of life.
Deb

My name is shipwreck and I am
alone in the dark drifting in
the black murkiness without proper
navigational equipment. I tried to steer towards
land ho! But I lost my way AGAIN!!
Deb

I closed my eyes and wished on the black
star that I always see when I turn my mind
off to life and its complex patterns. The biological
capabilities
that I once held dear have chosen to deny me
any peace with which to process the disturbance in my
soul. A soul so infected and putrid with hate that I laugh
aloud with euphoria when my flesh crawls and stings. I don't
care
if you don't understand my misery. I don't care if you can't
grasp my discomfort. I don't care! I just don't care!
Deb

Deeper is better because all of the garbage and rage spew forth with
a vengeance. I am the driver of my vehicle of insanity and loneliness tonight
does anyone else want to ride on the dull edge of my razor coaster and
participate in the extreme slice of life known to many who constantly claw their
way into a society blinded by the light who resort to cruel and unusual
punishment upon themselves. Welcome to my world, a world once filled with the
laughter of an innocent child only to be replaced with horrific events that control
my mind set. I want freedom from the benevolence that holds me hostage, I think
I want death!
Deb

Tonight I celebrate the death of the illusion of my life. I never asked for more than
I was worth, yet they keep saying that I am over qualified. I paid my dues and
tribute to those who cut before me. I don't want to cut again but somehow the
dark forces move me like the wind in a storm and saturate my arms with bloody
passion.
Deb

The 1st day of March is self injury awareness day. This is a day for soul searching and decision making. If you have discovered someone or you are personally dealing with this destructive behavior DO SOMETHING ABOUT IT!!!!!!!!! You don't have to suffer anymore. It is time for you to appreciate yourself and celebrate your life.

If after reading this book you discover that you now have a name to fit what you have been doing to yourself for years, do not despair. There are several inpatients and outpatient treatment centers that can help guide you through your recovery process. Individual counseling and group counseling services are also available.

Consult your physician or local mental health center for self injury treatment, referrals and information.

If you are in the midst of a crisis call the self injury hotline!!!!!!!!

CPSIA information can be obtained at www.ICGtesting.com
Printed in the USA
LVOW131624210613

339728LV00002B/353/P